This one's for Deb and her future grandkids.
—T. L.

For my brother . . . unless he hits me with a big red ball.
—M. H.

Text copyright © 2020 by Tom Llewellyn
Illustrations copyright © 2020 by Mark Hoffmann

Book design by Melissa Nelson Greenberg & Iain R. Morris

Library of Congress Cataloging-in-Publication Data available.

ISBN: 978-1-944903-97-8 • Printed in China • 10 9 8 7 6 5 4 3 2 1

Cameron Kids is an imprint of Cameron + Company

Cameron + Company
Petaluma, California
www.cameronbooks.com

A IS FOR APPLE UNLESS...

TOM LLEWELLYN & MARK HOFFMANN

cameron kids

A is for Apple
unless you're being chased
by a bloodsucking vampire,
then A is for AAAAAAGGHHH!!!

Bb

B is for Ball
unless a ball just smashed
me in the belly,
then B is for barf.

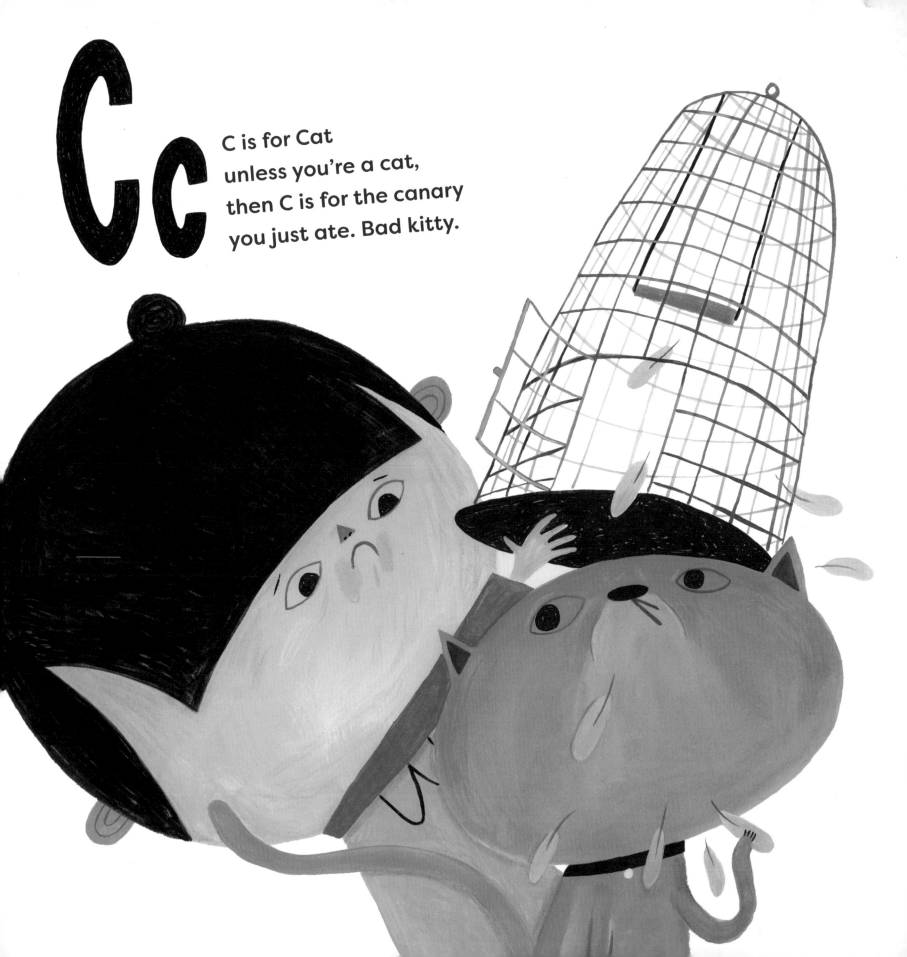

C c

C is for Cat
unless you're a cat,
then C is for the canary
you just ate. Bad kitty.

D is for Dog
unless you have a dog
and it's your job to
clean up after him,
then D is for doo-doo.

E e

E is for Elephant,
but if you have an elephant
instead of a dog, then E is for
extremely large shovel.

F is for Frog
unless you had beans for dinner,
then F is for a smelly noise that
rhymes with art.

Gg

G is for Glass,
but if someone just made a smelly noise that rhymes
with art, then G is for, "Geez! Why do you always blame me?"
It was probably the dog.

Hh

H is for Hat
unless you're sitting next to the
person (or dog) who made a smelly
noise that rhymes with art, then
H is for hold your breath.

Ii

I is for Ice Cream,
and if you scream loud
enough (and long enough),
you'll probably get some.

Jj

J is for Jam,
but if you don't have any jam,
then just take two pieces of
bread and jam them together.

K k

K is for Kangaroos.
Kangaroos are cute unless your
kangaroos know karate,
then K is for KA-POW!

L is for Lambs,
which are cute.
But L might be for lamb
chops, which are delicious,
especially if you're a wolf.

Mm

M is for Monkey
unless you have mountains of money.
Then M can be for whatever you want.
It can even be for apple if you're rich enough.

Nn

N is for Nose
unless you just picked your nose, then
N is for nasty, you nasty nose picker.

Oo

O is for Orange
unless you already knew that,
then O is for, "Oh, that's so obvious."

P p

P is for Pee,
and P is the strongest letter
in the alphabet. Even
Superman can't hold it.

Q is for Queen.
Even queens have
to pee sometimes.
And poop, too.

R is for Ring.
If you're in love with a queen,
you should give her a ring.
But you should probably wait until
she comes out of the bathroom.

S is for Snake
unless your sister is afraid of
snakes and screams a lot,
then S is for "Shhhh!!!"

Tt

T is for Tree.
Tell your sister you put your snake away. It's safe for her to come down from the tree now.

Uu

U is usually for Umbrella, but it should be for undies. If you ever have to choose between undies and an umbrella, choose the undies. Because you can go to school without an umbrella.

V is for Violin, but if that ball smashes me in the stomach one more time, then let's say it's for vomit. I'm going to go before I get hit by that ball again.

Ww

W is for Watch, as in, watch me find that kid who keeps hitting me with the ball.

X is for X-ray
unless it's for xylophone.
But that's it. With X, it's
either one or the other.

Y is for Yo-yo
or yak liver with yam sauce.
Yuck.

Z z Z is for Zoo and
Zebra and Zipper
unless we're
all done.

Then Z is for Zee End.

TOM LLEWELLYN is the author of several middle-grade novels. This is his only picture book unless he writes another. He lives with his wife and four kids in Tacoma, Washington.

MARK HOFFMANN is an award-winning children's book author/illustrator and fine artist whose books include *Poop*. He lives in southern New Hampshire with his wife and son.